For Nathan and Dina and for their parents.
— *S.T.*


For Harriet and Jack and our model Fox Terrier, Maud.
— *P.C.*

# THE ELEVATOR MAN

## BY STANLEY TRACHTENBERG
## ILLUSTRATED BY PAUL COX

Eerdmans Books for Young Readers

Grand Rapids, Michigan • Cambridge, U.K.

The Elevator Man wears a maroon uniform with brass buttons. His cap has a shiny black bill to keep the sun out of his eyes. Most of the time, though, he stands next to the elevator in Nathan's building.

When the Elevator Man stretches, he can almost touch the top of the cab with his fingers. Sometimes he lifts Nathan up even higher, all the way to the ceiling.

The Elevator Man dreams of becoming a doorman.
He would wear white gloves and pull at them — first one,
then the other — to make sure they fit. Then he would wave and
taxis would turn around and pull up in front of the building.

The Elevator Man pictures himself greeting people by touching his cap with one white-gloved finger. "Maybe one day . . ." he says, and looks away.

White gloves make Nathan think of Mickey Mouse.

Running the elevator seems important enough for anyone. That's what Nathan wants to do when he grows up.

Every morning Nathan's father lets him ring for the elevator. First, though, Nathan makes sure there is no fire on the landing. If there is, he will have to use the stairway. When you live on the fifth floor, stairs are no fun, especially for Nathan's father. He always talks about getting more exercise but has to lie down for a while after he does.

Nathan watches the pointer that shows where the elevator is. When it reaches his floor, there's a grinding noise. Then the Elevator Man yanks open the door.

"Tell him to hold it!" Nathan's father shouts from somewhere inside the apartment.

"My dad will be out right away," Nathan says to the Elevator Man.

But his father always has to finish doing something, like finding his keys or answering the phone. That takes a lot longer than right away!

On other floors, people in a hurry to get to work lean on the buzzer.

The Elevator Man just smiles. His smile lets Nathan know
he won't move until his father comes. When his father finally
does arrive, the Elevator Man slides the scissors gate shut.

They are sure to get dark looks when the elevator stops to
pick up people who have been waiting.

Inside the elevator cab, light spills over wooden panels. In
one of the panels a telephone is hidden. The Elevator Man
explains it's to call for help if the elevator gets stuck.

Nathan wonders who is on the other end of the phone.
How long would it take before they could unstick everything?
He hopes operators are standing by.

When Nathan gets home from school, sometimes no one else is around. The Elevator Man lets him sit on a fold-out stool in front of the controls and run the elevator.

Nathan turns the handle to the right to make the car go up. To the left it goes down. When he wants to stop, he brings it to the middle.

Nathan keeps his eye on the pointer above the door. Even so, he sometimes stops a little too high or a little too low. Then the Elevator Man shows him how to go very slowly so that the elevator comes out even with the floor.

One day Nathan sees a sign next to the elevator:

*Starting Monday, this elevator will be out of
service while it is being modernized. During
this period please use the service car.
We appreciate your patience.*

> C. Gumpert
> Building Superintendent

To get to the service elevator, Nathan has to use a door in his kitchen. The door opens to a small landing between apartments.

On Monday, he rings for the service elevator. When it comes, the Elevator Man isn't there.

Instead there's someone who wears a blue work shirt. The shirt has the word "MAINTENANCE" stitched in red over the pocket. The man has a stern look. Nathan often sees this look on the faces of substitute teachers.

He doesn't let Nathan run the elevator.

"The insurance won't let us," he says. "If something happened, the building would be sued."

Nathan isn't sure what that means. It doesn't sound good.

When his father calls to hold the elevator, the maintenance man says he can't wait and shuts the door.

*They have to do something about that insurance*, Nathan thinks. He wishes the Elevator Man would come back.

Meanwhile, Nathan doesn't ride down with his father anymore.

Weeks go by, and still the elevator isn't fixed.

Nathan asks his parents why it's taking so long.

"They have to replace the rollers," his father explains. "If they

don't have any in the warehouse, it takes longer to get them."

"What happened to the rollers?" Nathan wants to know.

His father seems to be thinking it over.

"The rollers . . ." he begins but can't finish. "The rollers . . ."

Nathan knows he was going to make something up.

His mother just smiles and shakes her head.

That means she doesn't know either.

One day Nathan sees that the "Out of Service" sign is no longer there.

That must mean the elevator is working again!

But what happened to the pointer? In its place is a strip of numbers. They blink on and off, one after the other. They make Nathan dizzy.

He presses the down button. It stays lit but he doesn't hear anything. Not a sound.

He presses it again. Then several more times.

Still no buzz to let him know anyone can hear the signal.

Suddenly the door to the elevator opens from the middle. There is no gate. Instead of one door there are two, one behind the other. The doors look like a sandwich with nothing between the bread.

Nathan steps inside.

The Elevator Man isn't there.

No one is.

Then the door closes even though he hasn't touched anything. Boxes of light spray down through a tic-tac-toe grille like the one in Nathan's kitchen.

The first thing he notices is that the folding seat has been taken away. So has the telephone. The wood panels are gone too. The elevator walls are polished metal.

A sign on the wall shows the car limit is 3,500 pounds. So there was one more thing to worry about. Nathan weighs only sixty pounds. But what if he were to bring his bicycle? Or if someone very big were to get on with him?

The worst thing is that the handle that lets him work the controls is gone. Instead, there is a panel with a button for each of the floors. There are also other buttons Nathan isn't sure about.

One is yellow and has the word "Call" written on it. Another in red says "Emergency."

Nathan reaches up to touch one of the buttons, the one that has an "L" on it. He hopes it means "Let Me Off."

Nathan hears a humming sound. It doesn't feel like he is going anywhere. He hears a steady beep, which means maybe he is.

He misses the wood panels and the telephone.

He misses the pointer that showed what floor you were on.

Most of all, he misses the Elevator Man. He misses his maroon uniform and the cap with a shiny bill.

Then the door opens. Nathan looks out into the lobby.

He can't figure out how he got there.

As quickly as he can, Nathan runs out of the elevator.

Outside he can see the doorman. He is blowing his
whistle and waving for a cab.
He is wearing white gloves.

When he turns around, Nathan's eyes grow wide.

It's the Elevator Man!

"Can I get you a cab, young man?" he asks.

Nathan laughs and shakes his head.

"I don't think so," says Nathan. "But can you take me back upstairs?"

"Don't have to," the Elevator Man says. "*You* can be the elevator man."

Nathan doesn't quite believe him. "Are you sure the rollers are fixed?" he asks.

The Elevator Man is sure.

"But how will the elevator know where to stop?" Nathan asks.

"Just press the number of the floor you want," the Elevator Man says.

Nathan looks to make sure he means it. "Just press 5?" he asks. "All alone?"

The Elevator Man nods.

Nathan looks up at the Elevator Man — the Doorman! — who smiles and points to the lobby with a wave. He understands that from now on, things will be different.

*Well, maybe not completely different,* Nathan decides. Then
he heads toward the elevator to begin his new job.

Published in 2009 by Eerdmans Books for Young Readers
an imprint of Wm. B. Eerdmans Publishing Co.

Wm. B. Eerdmans Publishing Co.
2140 Oak Industrial Dr. NE, Grand Rapids, Michigan 49505
P.O. Box 163 Cambridge CB3 9PU U.K.

www.eerdmans.com/youngreaders

Manufactured in China

09 10 11 12 13 14 15    9 8 7 6 5 4 3 2 1

**Library of Congress Cataloging-in-Publication Data**

Trachtenberg, Stanley.
The Elevator Man / by Stanley Trachtenberg ; illustrated by Paul Cox.
p. cm.
Summary: When the elevator in a building in the 1950s is modernized,
a young resident misses the operator.
ISBN 978-0-8028-5315-8
[1. Elevators — Fiction. 2. Elevator operators — Fiction. 3. Apartment houses — Fiction.]
I. Cox, Paul, 1957- ill. II. Title.
PZ7.T6825El 2009
[E]--dc22
2008031737